THE CUP

AND

KETTLE CORNER

Writings of the Named and Unnamed

Amy R. Roberge

Copyright

Copyright © 2024 Amy R. Roberge. All rights reserved.
No part of this publication may be reproduced, stored or transmitted in any form or by any means without written permission from the publisher. Unauthorized copying, posting to a website, or distribution by other means is prohibited.

Certain identifying details have been changed to protect the privacy of individuals, except where permission has been granted.

All photographs and these writings along with the cover design were created and published by Amy R. Roberge

*To
204*

CONTENTS

Permission Granted

Listening As A Spiritual Practice

Others Focused

Holy Places Everywhere

Named And Unnamed

Small Things

Impermanence

Leave The Light On

The Grace Of Readiness

Join Me At The Meadow

Being Here Now

In Restless Pursuit

Before And After

The Language Of Bells

All Things Wild

The Mystery Of Life

Finding Gold

Look Out Any Window

The Giving Tree

Reverence

The Crooked Door

Blanket

Home For The Holidays

Permission Granted

The soft notes of piano music echo around me as I hold
tight to a snow globe that now fills the span of
both hands. The end of a long day welcomes me at the
window in this dimly lit kitchen, here in an old
town in New England. The holiday season still speaks to
me in its quiet way, the wonder held forever in
the snow globe that I now hold.
This new year, with its endless possibilities and unknown
destinations, has now arrived for each one of
us.
How I wish for just a moment to find myself inside this
globe.
The lone audience of the display of the glimmer of snow
that now falls gently around me, landing in my
hair and along my shoulders.

Here in this place, my face turned upward to catch a
glimpse of that which
is home to this slivery etched snow that now falls steadily.
Home. Maybe some could say it's not a place
but a primal sense of safety. A natural beingness with no
question of yourself or worrying about where
you are going or what it is all for; feeling safe and free.
The new lies beyond the known, and as we settle into our
own feeling of home, know that you are safe
and free to be open to the possibilities of the unknown. Our
adventures will always lead us back to this
place within ourselves of home again and again.

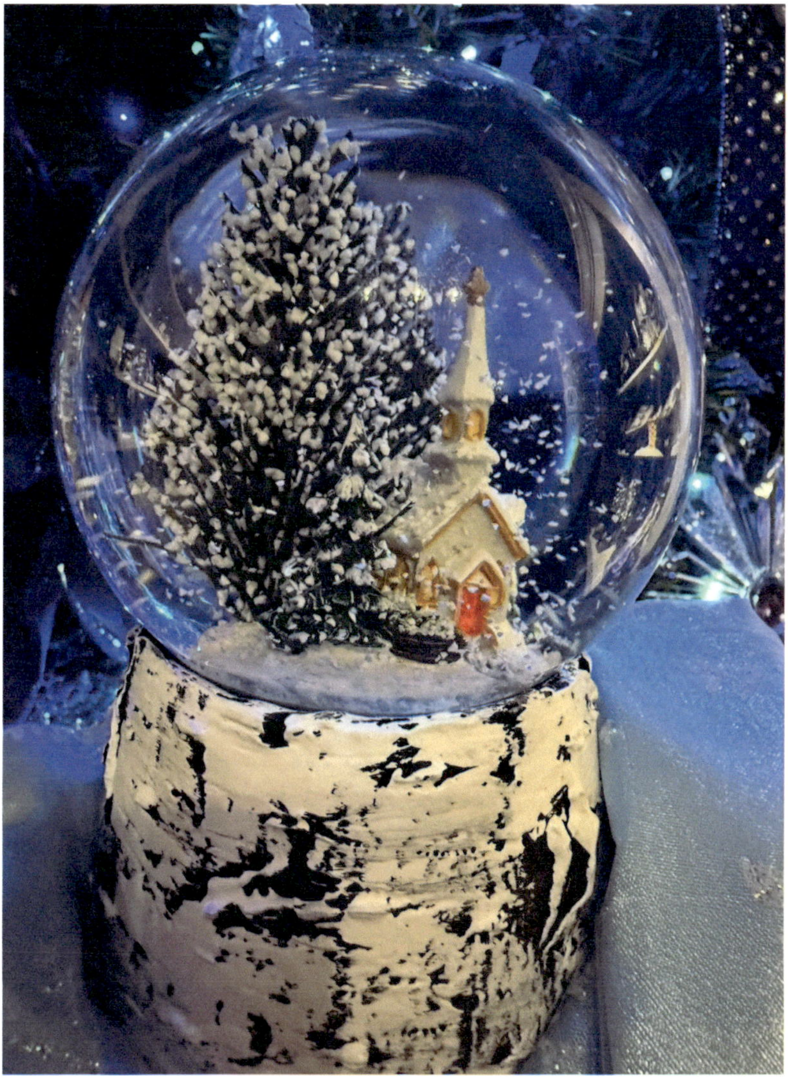

Listening as a Spiritual Practice

The art of storytelling is as old as time itself. We were brought into this world with a steadfast love of effervescent stories that gave life to the world we live in today.

We have long given audience to the rich details of our daily occurrences, chasing the particulars that tell the story of our world.

The first duty of love is to listen. Has it been by choice? Or Inherent social expectation? What can we glean if we listen carefully? The subtlety of a message is unspoken.

The Native Americans have a saying that says, "The only true communication is without words." I invite you to remember the vastness of a time spent in the woods or any other place where we can reminisce about listening as a spiritual practice.

Can you remember an exchange with someone where you could feel their love and concern for you just by their eyes? Your child or a cherished one apprehensive without mentioning why?

Know that one of the greatest gifts you can give is that of your time. Through the gift of your time, you have reached out your hand to join another person in the trenches of a difficult moment.

Words can hinder us at times and fall short of what's in our hearts.

Listening as a spiritual practice widens our landscape to be a better person for ourselves and for one another.

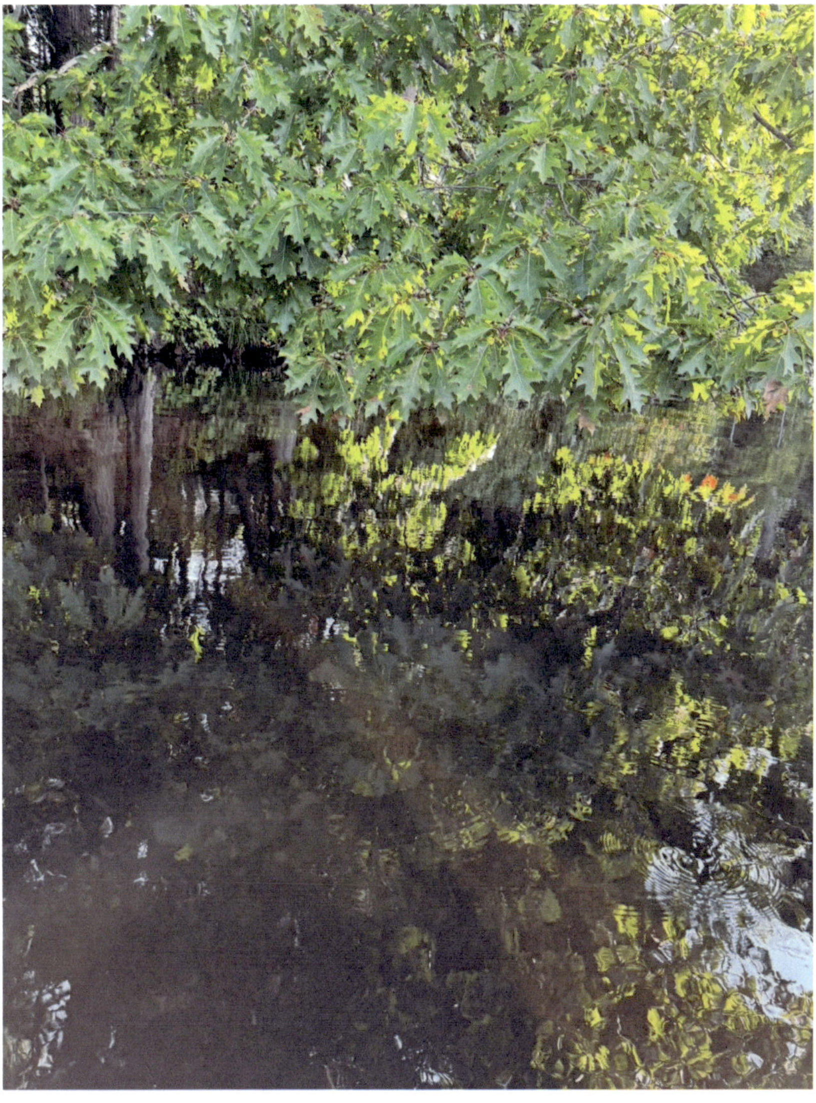

Others Focused

The brightly colored box gives way from my rushed efforts to open it, spilling pastel-colored candy hearts across our worn maple table here in a cozy kitchen in an old town in New England. My eye catches a few of the two-word sentiments that endear each candy, and with renewed hope, I begin again, filling the now-freed hearts into gifting bags so that they, too, can bring a smile.

We all have lasting memories of filling out our Valentine's Day cards as children before sending them on their way to home-crafted boxes decorated with the brightest of pink and red. How nice it is to be thought of. To think that someone took time from the busyness of their day to really thank you for leaving a lasting impression of the time spent with you. Our hearts swell in these moments and are assured of the gratitude that now flows both ways… Wishing you many candied hearts and Valentine's Day blessings.

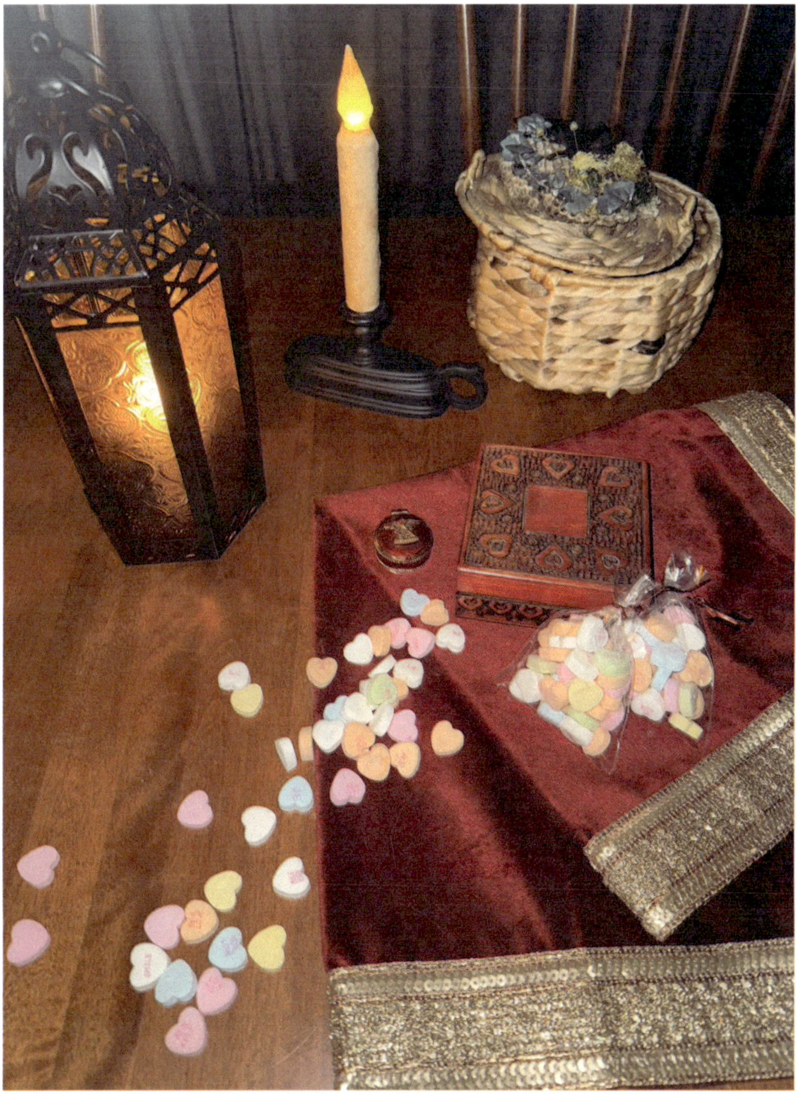

Holy Places Everywhere

How blessed we are to live in a place that is ever-changing. Our seasons, our day-to-day weather, and even the natural world around us.
How nature seems to follow the rhythms of our world so effortlessly.
There is beauty all around us, in small moments and big, in its busyness and stillness. Our perception of these pieces of time makes up our life experiences, gifting us with their memory.
Can you remember when someone reminded you of something you said that left you in awe, but you have no memory of this and its impact on the other person? Have you ever found yourself watching something unfold, finding the beauty within it, and feeling compassion?
We gift the world with these moments.
Holy places are painted from our awareness of what we take notice of and how we can create them for others.
Our heart grants its worthiness and takes notice that there are holy places everywhere.

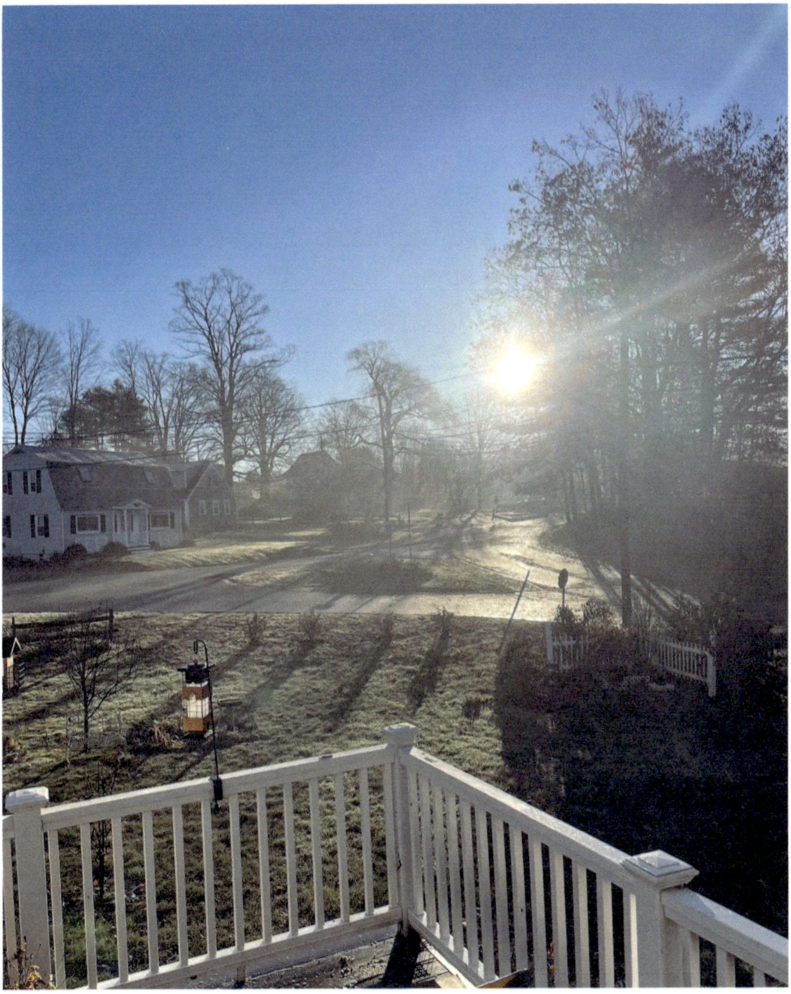

Named and Unnamed

My mind drifts for a bit as I stop short to take in the view from the corner window in a cozy kitchen here in New England. The early morning light changes by the minute as nature remains undecided about its offerings for this day. The stove softly hums as I watch the goings-on across this stretch of property. A neighbor hurries from tree to tree, collecting buckets that will later yield gallons of the sought-after New England maple syrup.
There are several varieties of maple trees; of those, I know none. I have never been very good at remembering names…I am, though, in envy of those who have a name that speaks of much more when spoken.
 Our names are timeless pieces of our life history that are stitched together to tell our story. They say, too, that to say the name of those departed is that they will never be forgotten. There are the unnamed things, too. The steam from the sunrise on a cold morning in March, the endless stretch of time in the middle of the night, and the silence that fills the conversation between two friends sitting on a drafty porch overlooking the meadow in winter. There is beauty in both named and unnamed things.

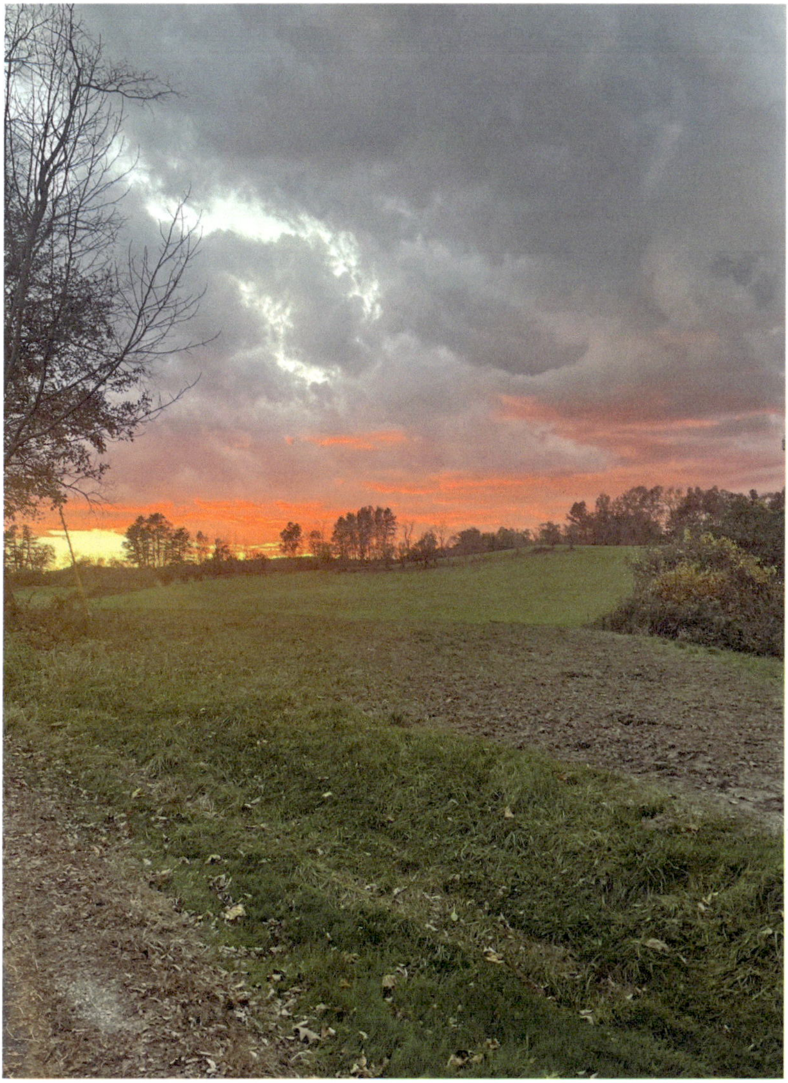

Small Things

The afternoon has gotten away from me this cool April day as I steal a glance at the clock that hangs just beyond our kitchen in an old town here in New England. My bread pans sit in wait by the fire and heat radiating from our pellet stove, promising my favorite oatmeal spice bread by evening.

Just the other day, I came across a recipe to make a 90-second bread…using the microwave and then finishing with the help of the toaster. I thought that a new way of doing something and small things could be great. I probably won't make the remkin bread again, but I was left with the feeling that I at least tried something new. They say the new lies beyond the known. It is difficult for some to try something new…or even do something differently. We can start small, and small things can be great.

FARMHOUSE MARKET
★ BUTTER · CHEESE · MILK ★

Impermanence

The last light of a waning afternoon calls to me as I pause for a moment, catching the last of the light from the far window of a cozy kitchen here in New England.
The ethereal ache is still fresh, as I am still missing our tree that no longer fills the view just outside the framed window pane. How many times my world righted itself with just a glimpse of a lone sprightly tree that leaned oddly to the right. My faithful friend, branches swaying as if giddy from my presence, noticed from the far window. Spanning years of countless times filling me anew, whether wary from mothering my children or seeking to watch the last light of the day streaming in from the late day sun. The majestic tree whose inhabitants returned each season to call it home and the wild roses that bloomed each year under the perfect balance of sun and shade. Its labyrinth of branches spanned the sky, casting shadows in the darkness of night. Our tree is no longer, having lost amid the weight of an ice and wind storm this past winter. I am left with the legacy of impermanence and its many lessons when having to tell the story of its demise. Change always comes when it's least expected, and we are almost never ready for it. But we can be prepared to know that change is complicated and has many layers to it. We make time our friend when we are patient with these layers and allow the pain and difficulty to work itself out. Our world will always help to right itself as my sprightly tree did for me by just taking a moment to see its beauty.

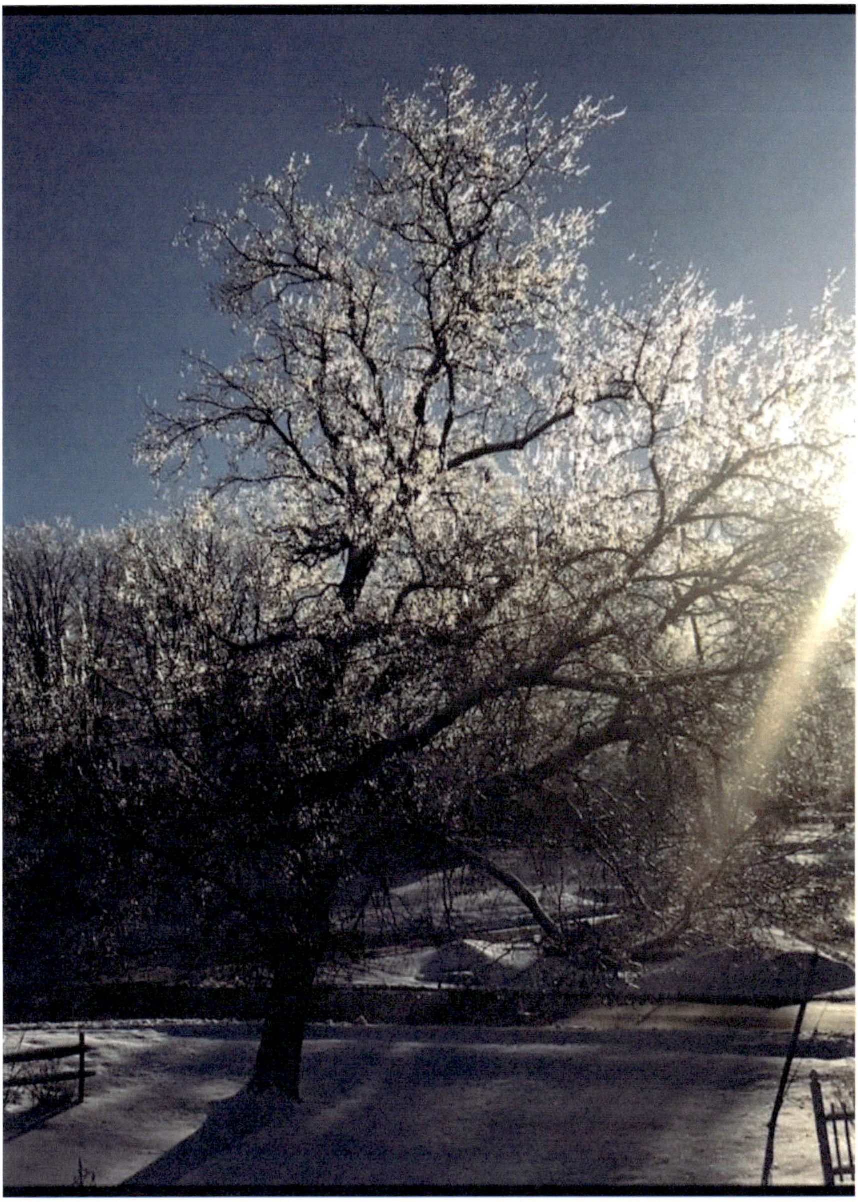

Leave the light on

A late morning mist rolls in as I rush to finish up my to-do's this early spring morning in an old town here in New England. A weather front has made its way up the eastern seaboard, commanding the attention of all in its path. High winds with more than just a seasonal rainfall are expected; with this, my hope is to see this grand display at a 19th-century lighthouse that is a cherished spot and perfect for viewing the ocean in wait of a storm. Some distance away, the lighthouse stands tall and ready. This day, it is the radiating light that is striking. The enormous revolving lens is light, beaming a soft velvet red that now pierces through gathering mist, leaving reflections of light now breaking in the building waves. It is this light, along with its beauty, that I will remember when I look back on the years of making this journey to the lighthouse before the rage of a storm. The light felt like a promise. A promise that all will be well, that we just have to look for the light.

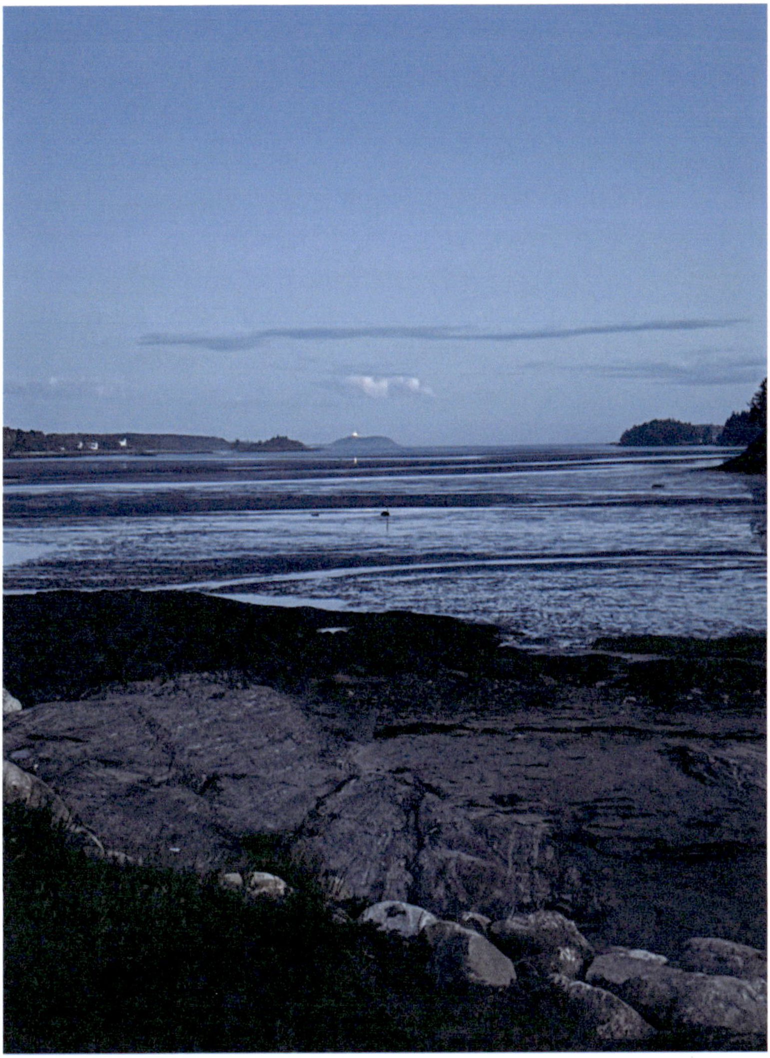

The Grace of Readiness

We love birdhouses. We have several that are patch-quilted on our shed that bear the same color as our home. If you look just off to the left from the far window of our cozy kitchen here in New England, you will be gifted each morning with the goings on of both our chickens as well as a spritely pair of songbirds. Quite the pair, working tirelessly to bring forth the next generation of the Chipping Sparrow. It is their subtle chirping woven into other unnamed chords that draw our attention to the window most mornings. A few moments were spent being witness to the necessary busyness of crafting a nest in the bright yellow, well-worn birdhouse that has housed new life every spring. Readiness requires internal adjustment, with a commitment to its equal, being prepared. We become acutely aware of an impending need to make these adjustments within ourselves at just the right times in our lives. Whether it be the movement, processing of fear, or coping with feelings of lack of control, we can call Grace for help arranging these unknowns. This Grace Of Readiness, through the art of preparedness, asks us to meet with our unknowns, arriving just as we are. We then can be ushered along with others like the Chipping Sparrow, boldly facing the next phase of our lives, or what I like to call the next adventure.

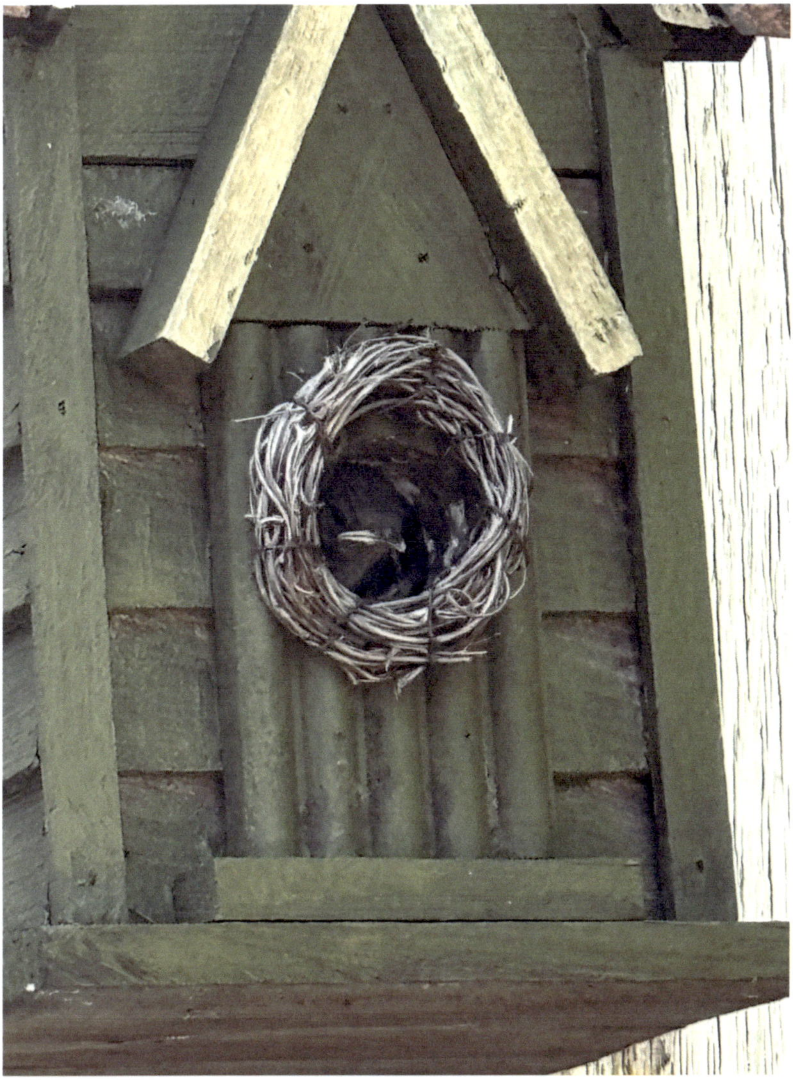

Join me at the Meadow…

This day, which holds no more significance than the day before, finds me here in a cozy kitchen in an old town in New England. My hand reaches without much thought to the pendant that hangs loosely around my neck. The wispy whites of a dandelion in its forever home, gently still within its sphere of resin. The life of a dandelion…Over a span of a month, it will bloom with the radiance of sunny yellow and is the first flower the bees will forage on when they venture out in early spring. Soon, the flower closes, readying the seeds that we see later as the wispy whites. Watch as the butterfly makes its way to the orange tiger lilies and how the black-eyed susan peaks out from the lupine with its brilliant colors. A warm breeze rushes through the meadow when you notice the echinaceas standing tall, swaying with the breeze. The invitation is always here, just a thought away; I am looking forward to sharing its time with you as well. A place with no time really. This gift of a wispy white was my invitation.

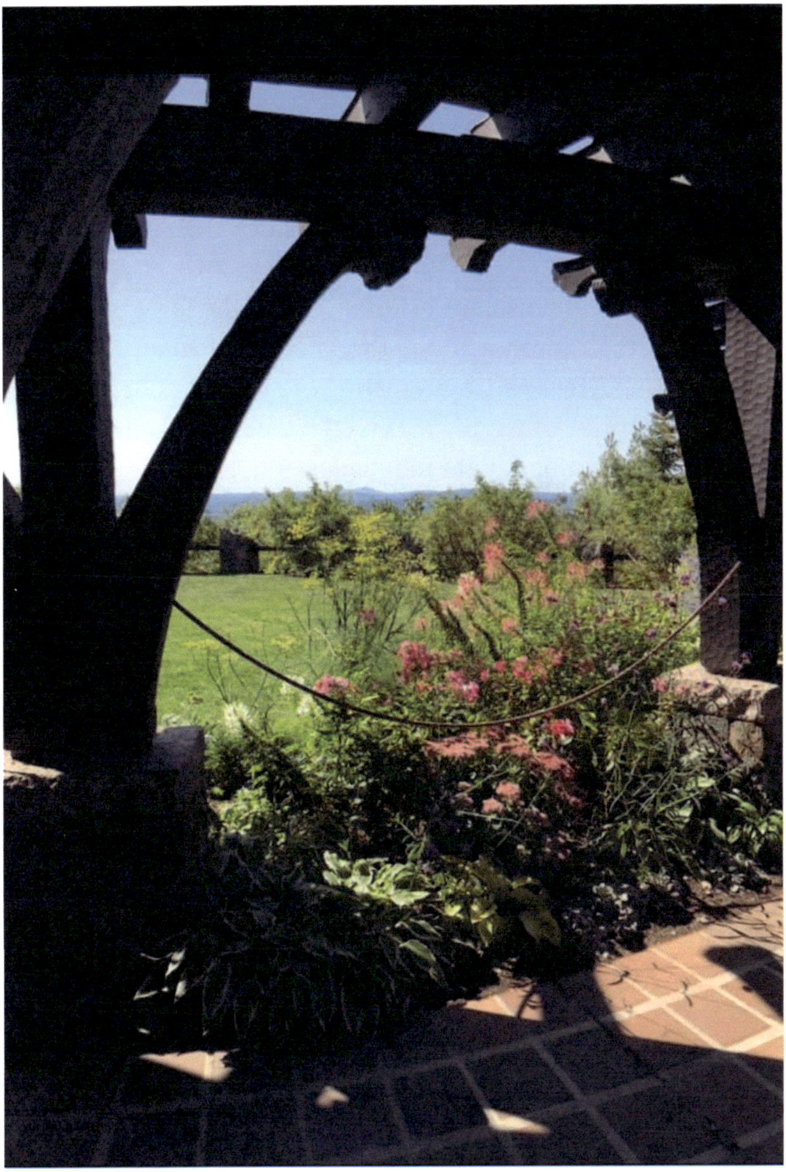

Beeing Here Now

The beginnings of a perfect day in our corner of what we call home.
Our bees show themselves briefly through the far window, balletic on their journey to the first blooms of June.
Every spring, we await, anticipating the show of our bees, with the surprise of having survived the perils of a hard winter. For a moment I am in wonder of the life of a bee. Life never intended us to be perfect; being in the messy middle is hard work. Yet we can move through something and come out the other side, which is not always the way we had hoped, yet we are still finding our way once again. I can be found this early morning in my favorite recliner, tissues within reach, another day of a relentless cold. There is a saying that says you can stand still, and life will continue to happen around you. My work has yet to begin for the day as I am still and quiet. Here, I am met with the beginnings of this perfect day. I am thankful I didn't miss it.

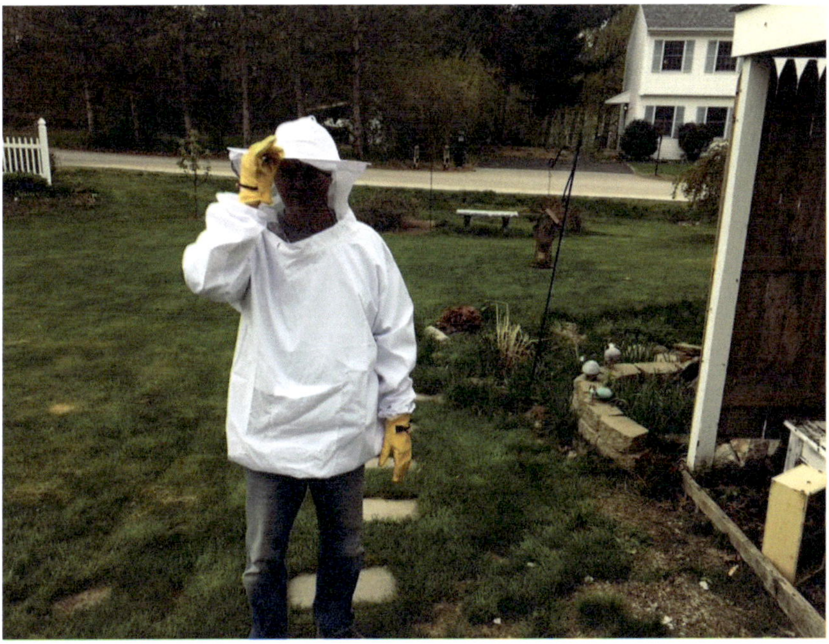

In Restless Pursuit

A geological creation known as The Balancing Rock can be found in the Tatnic region through a series of trails through the Great Works Land Trust. The scent of grey owl juniper fills the air on this cloudless day as I round the corner here in an old town in New England. This forest showcases the remnants of our most recent Ice Age, which deposited the massive rock that rests forever, still on its granite perch. This day, my attention is spread freely among the breeze that moves through the pine as it has done so many times before. This moment, now held in the quiet of the woods, will hold the memory of both the "seen and unseens" of my visit. I sense the assurance to take the time—the time to look up in restless pursuit, ponder the mystery of it, and let it take me where it may.
Soon, celebrations will be underway for this 4th of July along with the promise of picnics, bright displays of fireworks, and the backdrop of sounds of joy when the days are long and there is "no time" among visits with friends.

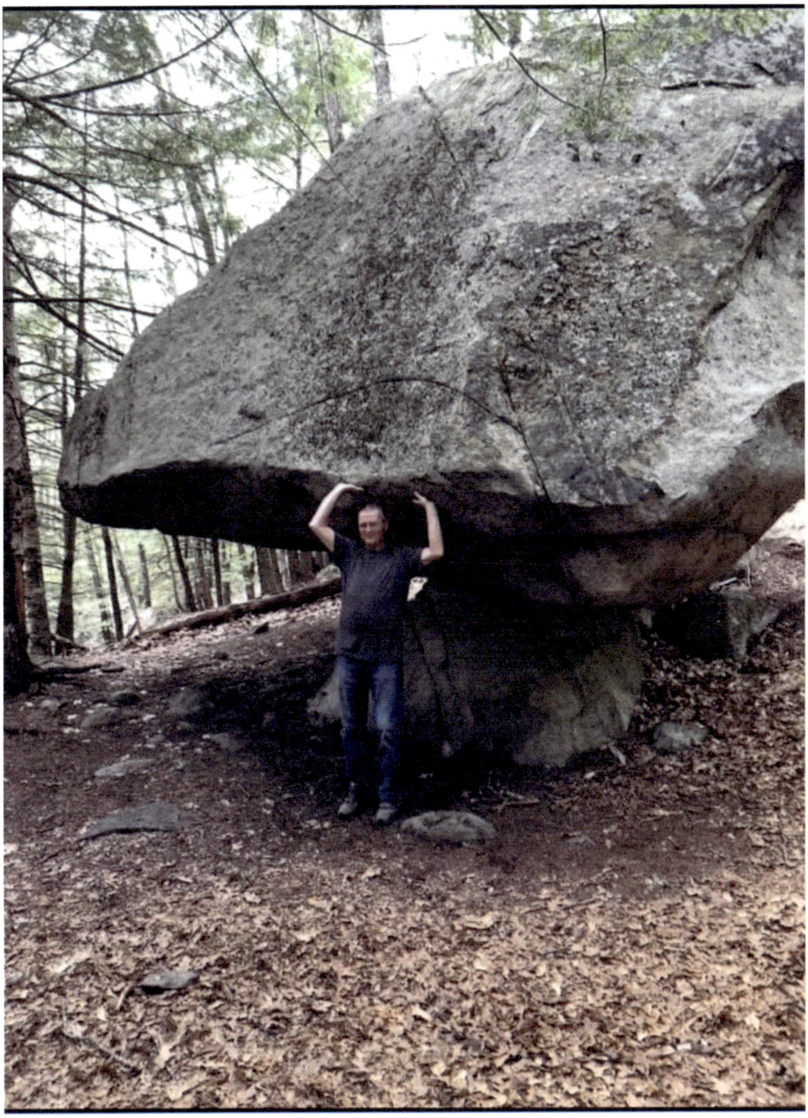

Before and After

A soft rain falls unnoticed if not for the rhythmic motion of my windshield wipers somewhere in an old town here in northern New England. A team of matching carriage horses holds my attention now; an Amish family making their way through to destinations that this summery day has called to them. I watch for a moment as one of the horses casts his head in the air to take in a full breath, his charge neatly arranged in the ebony carriage bearing the same color as he.

This place has called before and has been met with a quiet answer; those seeking rural life.

This place, where I have heard the loons call or looked up to see the bald eagle… Today, a wedding will take place, the joining of two people who will now take their first steps as one. At this same moment a room goes still, as the light changes from the day now clearing.

The sun, just as bright as if it were here the whole time. The resounding saunter of the carriage horses pull their charge across the road. I say a quiet prayer for the young couple as I think of how we all have our own before and afters, and of how far we have come as people, making the telling of the story of our own lives or the telling of what we see out there in front of us, just as rich.

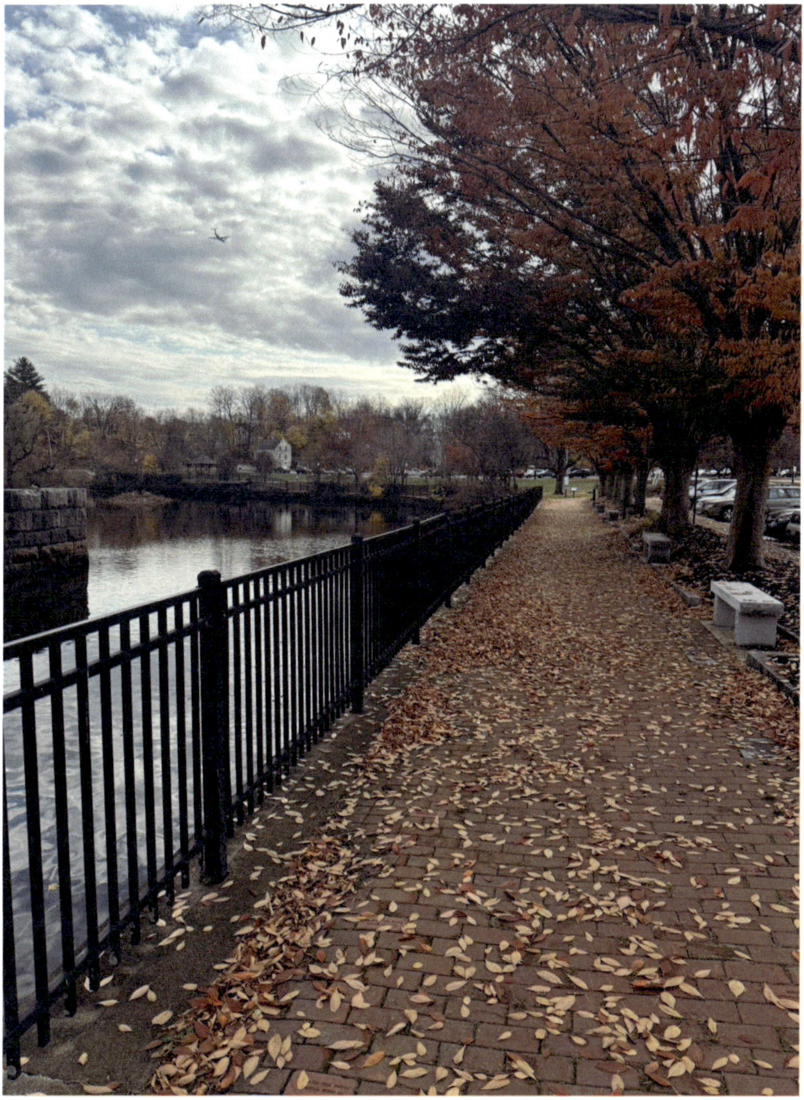

The Language Of Bells

The efforts of a hurried morning are hushed now that I have arrived. A place that will soon echo with cascades of ringing bells here in an old town in New England. The sun has gifted me with its steady presence, as if it, too, waits for the chiming of the bells.

Power has returned to our words in this life, and with them, their promised messages that can find us in the dark. What of the times, I wonder when two people share company without the spoken word, just the energy of life that moves freely between them. The words were there, having found no urgency as they found rest within the warmth of friendship.

In life, we see what we are asked to remember. It is the chiming of the bells now that brings me back to what I have waited so long for. The bells speak their own language, it seems…reminding us gently to listen with our hearts. They will join us there with gifts of joy as we bear witness to all things beautiful.

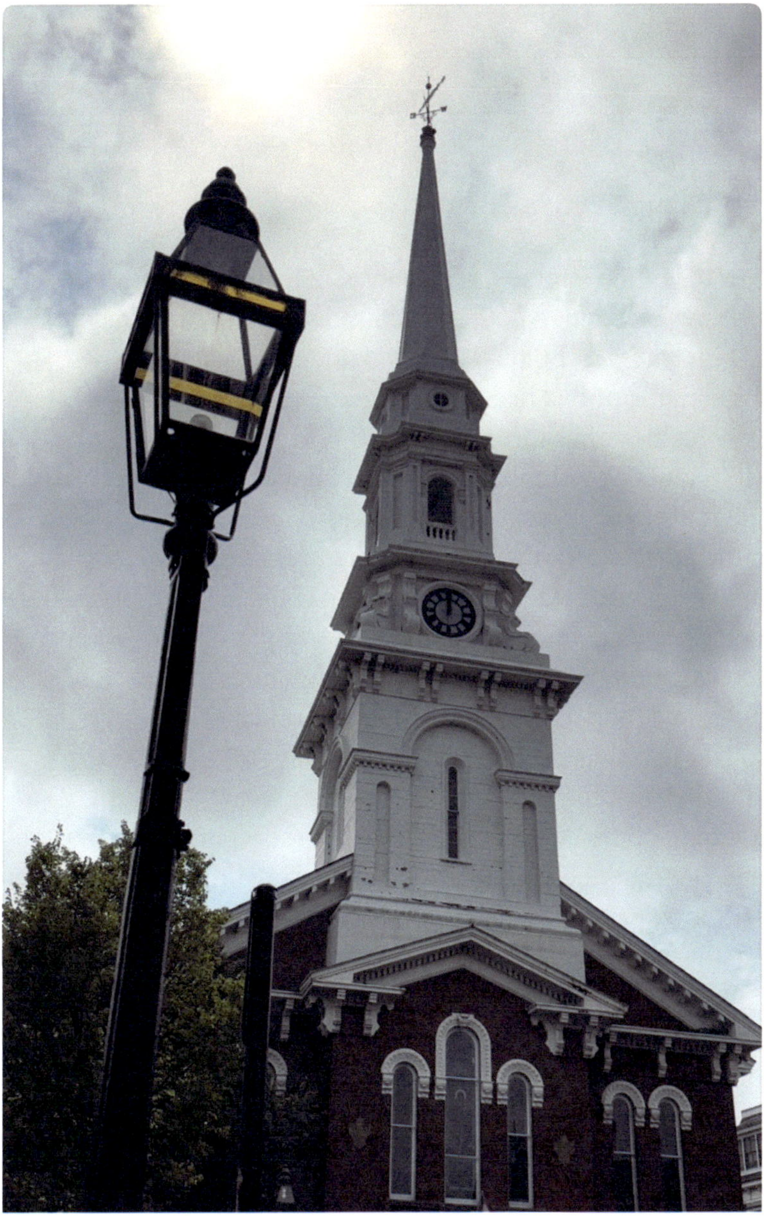

All Things Wild

A midsummer sun rests high noon in a cloudless sky here in New England. Another promised warm summer day and the busyness of both all things wild and of us, the inhabitants of this beautiful earth.
A container of my freshly canned raspberry jam lay open; I sit in quiet contemplation, willing heaping portions to make the journey from jar to my still-warm baked banana muffins. Raspberries are said to be invasive; they can grow new stems from roots that travel from the original plant. I once saw a stem maybe three inches high that had worked its way though a crack in a piece of granite, on this stem hung one lone red raspberry. On that midsummer day, I sat to rest just a short distance down on a granite stone stairway leading down to a river that I sometimes visit. For a moment, the beauty of the day and the sight before me had filled my heart. But now, it was the wild raspberry. I will forever now take notice of all things wild.

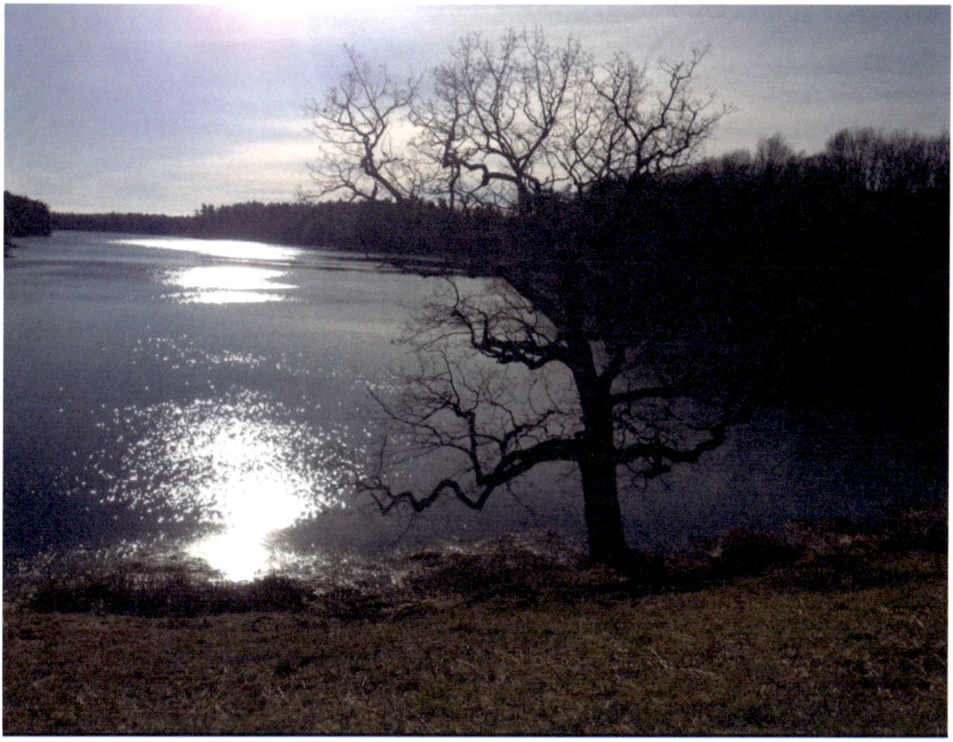

The Mystery Of Life

The cool wind of September has chased away the sun's rays this early morning in an old town in New England. I look up to assure myself of the sun's presence in its jealous sky, as if the clouds are lost to another tomorrow.

It is my favorite season of the year. I strain to hear the song of the birds, and I sometimes ponder the meaning of their message. As time passes, I have come to realize that it is in the wonder that holds the message.

As we journey through the seasons of our lives, it is said that the wisdom of these years makes us wiser…I wonder, too, if we have ever given up understanding the mystery of suffering, which is as big as the mystery of life itself. Each of our versions of these answers is what makes up the fabric of life, along with the beauty it holds for each of us. I challenge you to ponder the mystery that has captured your attention this day.

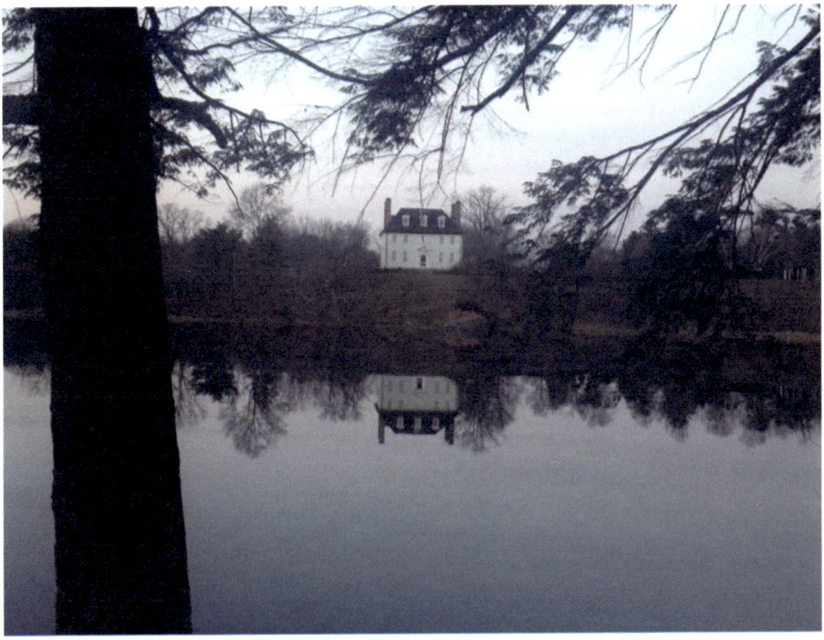

Finding Gold

Hues of late summer color make their way along the tree line in an old town here in New England.
A light breeze carries the promise of cooler days, the hallmark of the season to come.
In the morning sun, my eyes catch the glimmer of golden remnants in a small bottle resting in its forever home along the window pane here in our cozy kitchen. A gift, many years ago from its collector, the efforts of panning for gold!
My thoughts drift for a moment.. of rushing waters, swirling sand streaming along the collector's pan. The collector, hopeful, expectant, and even willing all that shimmers to find its way to them.
Wild and rebellious, the river, up for the challenge to keep hidden, this treasure of gold. Finding gold in one another shares the collector's efforts: often hidden, yet we are hopeful, expectant, and willing.

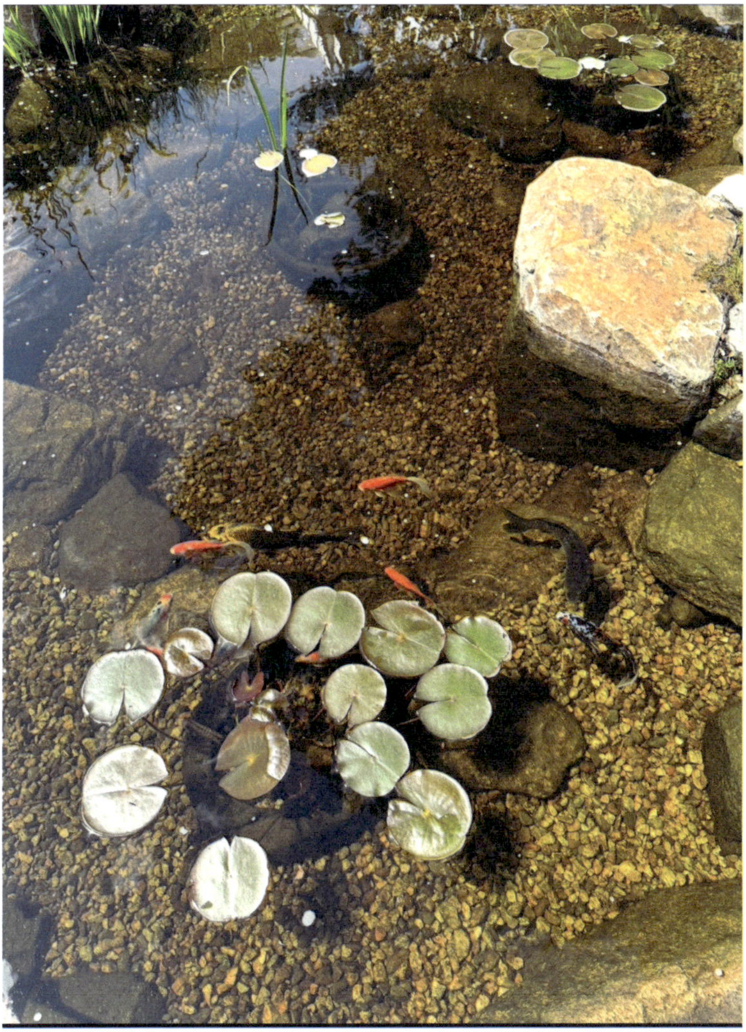

Look Out Any Window

The stillness is so quiet I almost miss the cue to look out my window, here in the busiest of rooms in the place I have called home in an old town in New England for just under a quarter of a century.
My best work has been birthed from this room in the quiet of morning… I search for something beautiful from the distance from where I dwell to out there that can be anywhere.
 I have wondered, when my gaze falls to the top of the highest of trees, am I the only one that ponders its life? The sway moments later bows as if to answer my query. The days and colors change, but the scenes out there pull at me differently now. I now see reverence and all that is sacred. Before, just bits and pieces of a puzzle.. and no place, time, or much thought was given to where these pieces were birthed and the life they now hold. Now, we can will time to pause for just a moment to carve out the piece we know will fit with our version of the world we wish to see. All is beautiful and sacred out there.

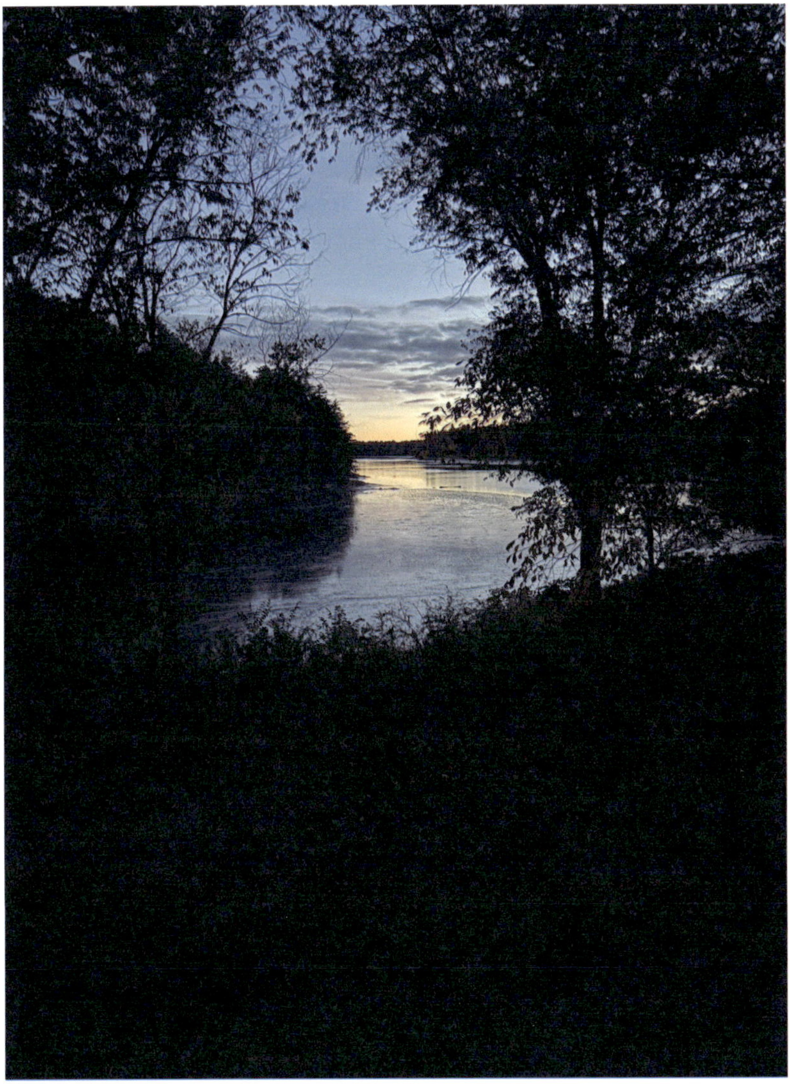

The Giving Tree

The last of the sun-filled promised days have yet to come out of hiding as our beautiful earth graciously welcomes the season of autumn. An unspoken language between the two makes itself known here in an old town in New England.
I watch from the far window of our cozy kitchen, a hint of how little concern the squirrel has of the many tomorrows to come as he rushes through a patchwork of leaves. Like all of the earth's charges, this squirrel has no concern of needing a coat, or where the next cool drink of water will be discovered. The leaves from this giving tree, now home to this squirrel, are imbued with colors: red, gold, and orange. An emollient to ease our weariness of the day. A light wind comes through the yard, and I watch as the leaves tumble to unknown destinations. The tree gave freely of all that it was with offerings of itself; the leaves, in months passed, offered a cool shade and soon will gift their shelter to the tiniest of creatures. Our life, too, falls under the orchestra of this flow. As we near a new season in our own lives, we know we are held lovingly by this same beauty. The natural flow and rhythm of life with its many shades of color and its lasting promise of ease that our needs will be met always.

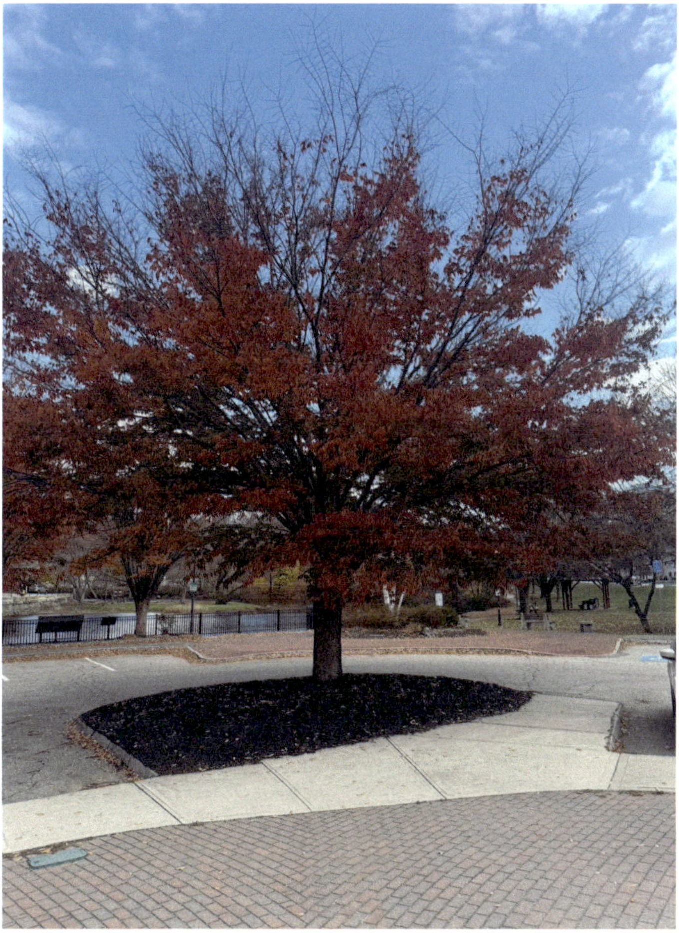

Reverence

 I yield to the end of this long day, willing my hot steaming tea to cool just a bit. Graced with the knowledge that tomorrow calls to be quite dreary, with offerings of icy rain that have yet to transform into the lightest of snow here in an old town in New England. The show of steam from my tea holds my attention now as I feel myself settle. My tea filled to the rim in its pale blue oversized mug with handcrafted feathers etched along its edges. My thoughts drift back to a memory… The hot August sun of Native American dancers dancing, the waft display of color of their regalia, the roaring sound of drums, and the dust kicked up from skilled dancers cast a soft glow.

An eagle feather falls from a headdress. In a moment's time, dancers had protectively encircled the feather that now lay still on the earth. There was no thought of time as they waited for their medicine man, who then gifted the ground with tobacco, bending with purpose to call home this revered feather of the beloved bald eagle. These stretched moments of displaced reverence of the eagle feather. In the native culture, the eagle and its feathers symbolize what is bravest, strongest, and holiest.

That just a feather could mean all these things. It is said that what you give attention to shows your reverence for it. In the season of Thanksgiving, I am left to my thoughts of what I hold reverent, having no thought of time to protect, honor, and give my love while being brave enough to gift the world displays of reverence.

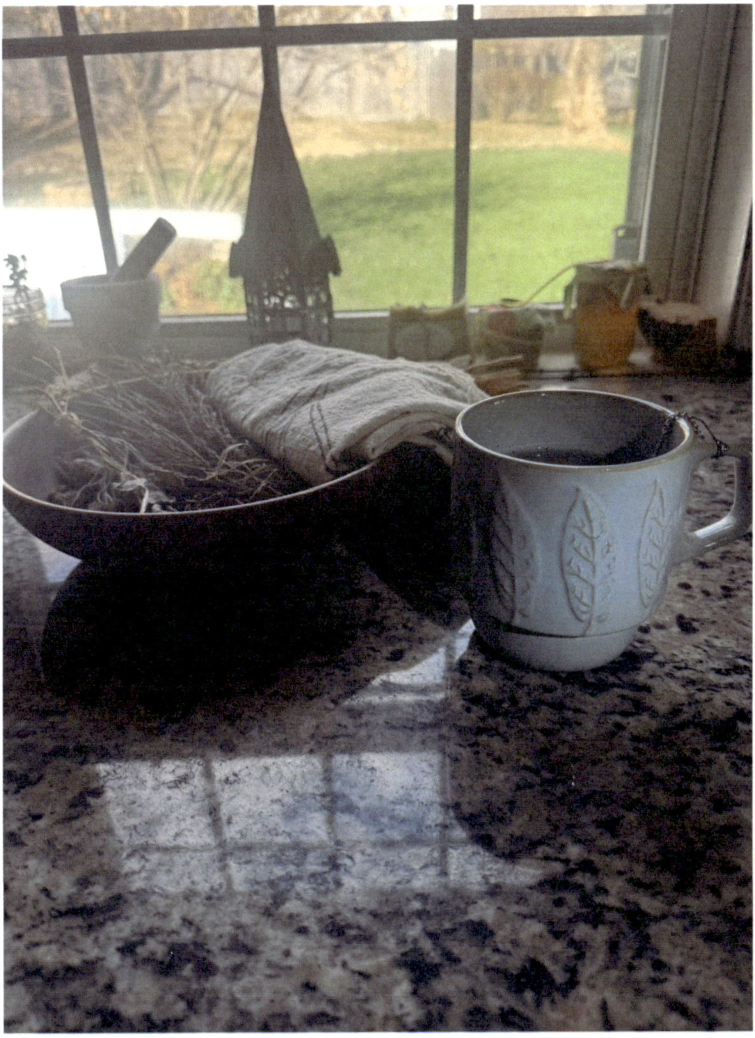

The Crooked Door

"There was a crooked man who walked a crooked mile…" The words of this early twentieth-century nursery rhyme stream through my memory as I catch a glimpse of the framed photograph that now hangs across the doorway of my home here in an old town in New England. Inspired by the iconic rows of crooked houses from the once prosperous merchant's village in Lavenham, England, the photographer felt called to photograph a few of the crooked doors from the still-standing multicolored half-timbered houses that lean at irregular angles. How endearing to feature imperfection and appreciate the unique character of even a door. These homes were built with green wood, and as they dried, they began to twist. I read once that our life can be thought of as a house and that the rooms can be thought of as the phases of our life. As you leave one room and enter another, you have entered another phase of your life. There is a choice here and a willingness to leave behind to step forward into the next, sometimes changing everything. The wonderment of what awaits us behind even a crooked door keeps us moving forward.

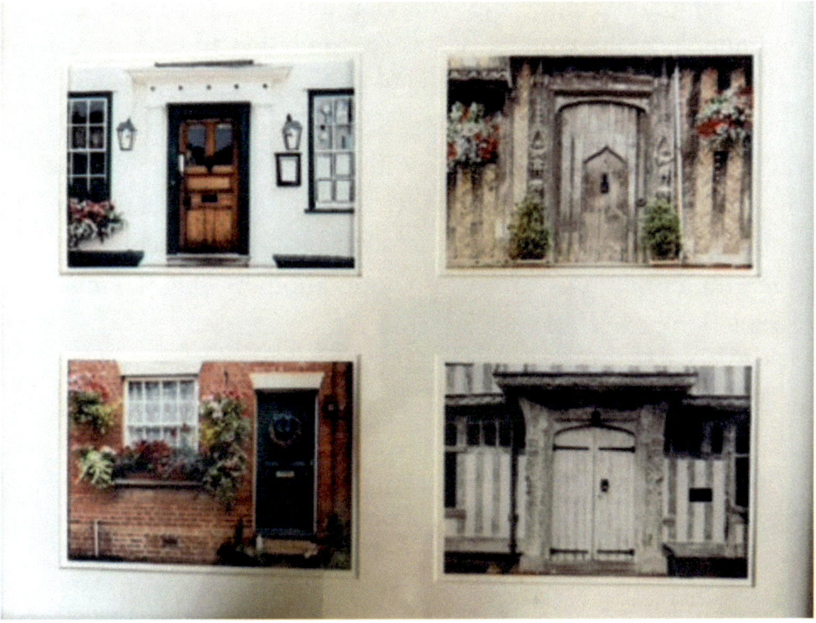

Blanket

The tasks of the day have long been tended to as I find rest at the window in our cozy kitchen here in an old town in New England. Heavy snow unrelenting but difficult to admonish as the wonder of this season holds all that shimmers. The light has changed and casts a long shadow across this stretch of floor. A patchwork quilt cascades along the length of my frame with its cream-colored edging that now lay gathered at my feet. This quilt was dreamed into the here and now many seasons ago. A lifetime yearning to quilt as each of my grandmothers had, having made look so effortlessly.

Before any idea is birthed, it is dreamed first. We breathe life into that which we create, from its tender beginnings to that of us being graced with its presence in the end. Beautiful things, to the tiniest of stitches to the crafted treasures we turn our attention to, some taking many hours. Some are gifted to those we love and care for, and others are kept for our own safekeeping and comfort. May the treasures of home and hearth be yours this Christmas.

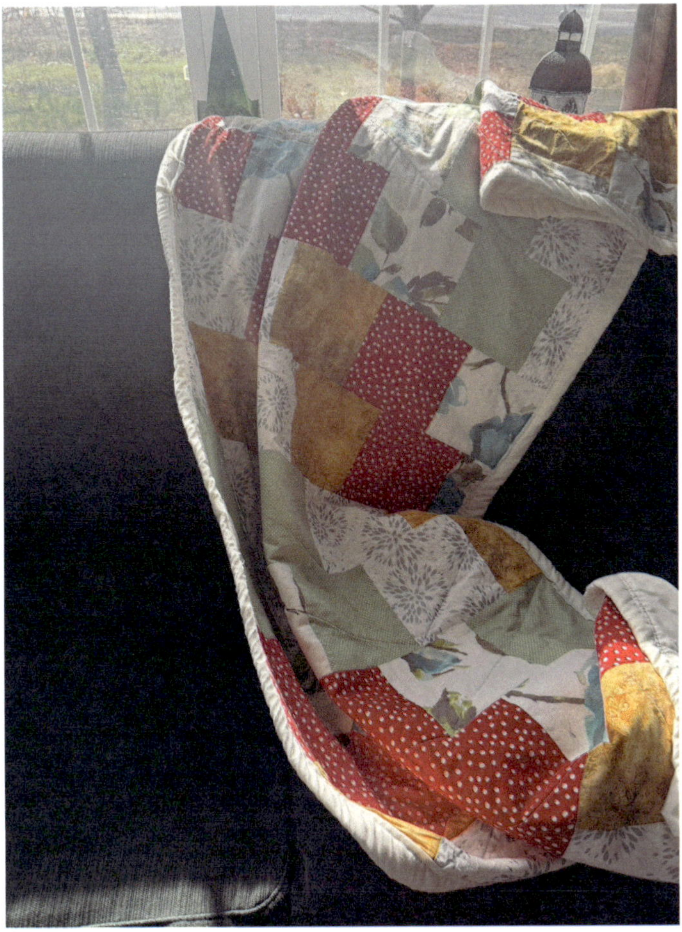

Home For The Holidays

I take a peek out the far window in a cozy kitchen here in an old town in New England on this cold winter day. Where the ocean meets the river, where the whistle from the railway sounds on the 3's, it's the coldest of days, I gather, when the call from the whistle is as clear as a winter day can be. Home For The Holidays is what we call the day long event that now is in its 20th year. The invitation is there this day, to enjoy a Christmas parade featuring the most unique of floats, leaving us with a smile that lingers. To the storefronts with an open door with the invite of a hot cocoa or a craft for the little one. Distant caroling will catch our attention soon with the rise and fall of our most beloved Christmas songs. Christmas trees of all sizes adorn doorways and from behind store windows, reflecting their soft glow. Along with the many memories that conjure up from the different smells that now fill the air. May merriment find you through a string of lights or a candy cane. It is this joy and simplicity that calls to the child you once were and who now rises eagerly. They wish to spend time with you here, in the season of Christmas, hoping to leave a smile that lingers.

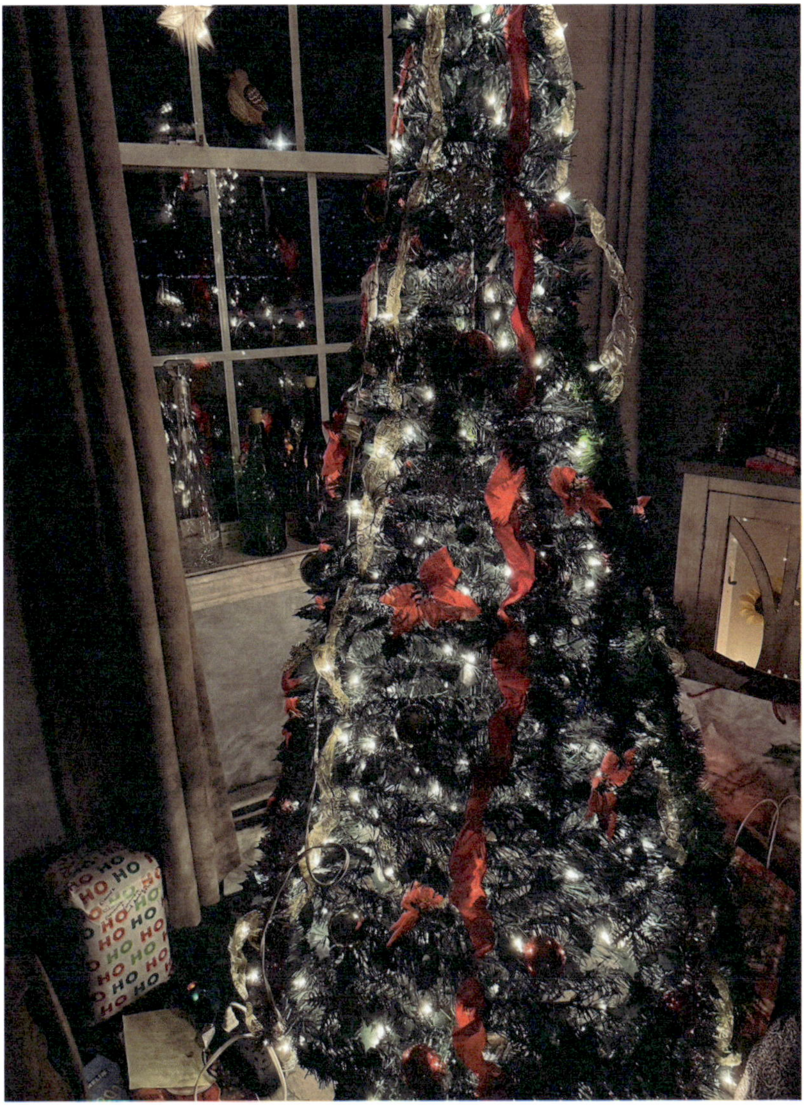

ABOUT THE AUTHOR

In her lifelong public service, Amy has served those in need in her work as a nurse, firefighter and most recently as a hospice chaplain and writer. Amy is also with those at the beginning of life in the NICU at a local hospital.

Amy lives on the seacoast of Maine, in a region close to both mountains and sea with her husband, daughter, dog and chickens.

Made in the USA
Columbia, SC
17 February 2025